2023

TEEN GUIDE TO THE SUPERNATURAL

HAL MARCOVITZ

ReferencePoint
Press®

San Diego, CA

YA
130
Marcovitz

About the Author

Hal Marcovitz is a former newspaper reporter and columnist and the author of more than two hundred books for young readers. He makes his home in Chalfont, Pennsylvania.

For more information, contact:
ReferencePoint Press, Inc.
PO Box 27779
San Diego, CA 92198
www.ReferencePointPress.com

32.95

Picture Credits:
Cover: Fer Gregory/Shutterstock.com (top left); Stasia04/Shuterstock.com (top right); Kiselev Andrey Valerevich/Shutterstock.com (bottom left); Anneka/Shutterstock.com (bottom right)

6: Sorin Colac/Alamy Stock Photo
9: Renphoto/iStock
11: FABIANO/SIPA/Newscom
14: Jon Bilous/Alamy Stock Photo
19: Nomad_Soul/Shutterstock.com
21: ©Look and Learn/Bridgeman Images
22: Associated Press
29: Perth Creative Studios/Shutterstock.com
30: Cristian Blazquez/Shutterstock.com
33: sdominick/iStock
39: Everett Collection/Shutterstock.com
41: MGM/Photofest
43: Pam Walker/Shutterstock.com
49: Dale O'Dell/Alamy Stock Photo
51: Moviestore Collection Ltd/Alamy Stock Photo
56: GUDKOV ANDREY/Shutterstock.com

LIBRARY OF CONGRESS CATALOGING-IN-PUBLICATION DATA

Names: Marcovitz, Hal, author.
Title: Teen guide to the supernatural / by Hal Marcovitz.
Description: San Diego, CA : ReferencePoint Press, Inc., 2024. | Includes bibliographical references and index.
Identifiers: LCCN 2023001013 (print) | LCCN 2023001014 (ebook) | ISBN 9781678205942 (library binding) | ISBN 9781678205959 (ebook)
Subjects: LCSH: Occultism--Juvenile literature. | Supernatural--Juvenile literature.
Classification: LCC BF1411 .M29 2024 (print) | LCC BF1411 (ebook) | DDC 130--dc23/eng/20230320
LC record available at https://lccn.loc.gov/2023001013
LC ebook record available at https://lccn.loc.gov/2023001014

CONTENTS

THE VAMPIRE TOURISTS

About 250,000 tourists from the United States and Canada visit the southeastern European nation of Romania each year. It is easy to see why. Many of Romania's cities and villages date back to medieval times, offering visitors views of churches, castles and other structures that are more than five hundred years old. In the wintertime, the country's range of alpine mountains offers some of the most thrilling skiing in Europe. Moreover, Romania borders the Black Sea, providing summertime tourists with some of the most beautiful beaches on the European continent.

But for many tourists none of that is the primary draw. According to statistics compiled by the Romanian government, about ten thousand Americans and Canadians visit the country each year with a single purpose in mind: they desire to see the birthplace of Count Dracula. Travel writer Rita Cook says:

> If you've read the book *Dracula* then you'll remember the English character Jonathan Harker who ate a meal at the Golden Krone Hotel in [the village of] Bistrita. . . . You can do that too and sleep at what is called the Castle Dracula Hotel in Bistrita. . . . If

you're looking for vampires and you've come this far, then you have to do it. The Castle Dracula Hotel is not very old, but it is built on the Borgo Pass at the site of the fictional Count's castle so it's just one more way to live the legend.[1]

DRINKING THE BLOOD OF HUMANS

As Cook explains, many people travel to Romania each year to visit the forests, castles, and villages that are woven into the story of Dracula, written by the nineteenth-century Irish author Bram Stoker. First published in 1897, *Dracula* tells the story of a Romanian count who is not human but rather a mythical creature known as a vampire.

Vampires survive by drinking the blood of humans who, if they are attacked by vampires, become vampires themselves. Vampires cannot endure sunlight—if exposed to the sun's rays, their bodies fade into a cloud of dust. Therefore, vampires only come out at night. They also cast no reflections in mirrors.

Since its initial publication, *Dracula* has remained one of the most widely read novels about vampires. The story has been adapted into numerous films over the years. And the tale of the bloodthirsty Romanian count has spawned other books, movies, and TV series about vampires. Indeed, the five films known as *The Twilight Saga*—a romantically themed series of movies featuring young lovers who also happen to be vampires—has earned the filmmakers more than $3 billion since the first movie in the series was released in 2008.

"If you're looking for vampires and you've come this far, then you have to [stay at Castle Dracula Hotel]."[1]

—Travel writer Rita Cook

POPULARITY OF THE SUPERNATURAL

The fact that so many fans flock to see movies about vampires—with some even prompted to travel to southeastern Europe hunting for the origins of Count Dracula's story—illustrates the popularity of the supernatural in modern culture. Vampires are

The medieval castle of Bran in Transylvania, Romania (pictured), is a popular tourist attraction due to its connection to the legend of Dracula. Large numbers of people travel to Romania each year to visit the forests, castles, and villages that are the setting for Bram Stoker's novel Dracula.

not the only supernatural creatures that have drawn interest over the years. Stories about ghosts and witches have been told for centuries. Many people visit fortune tellers to learn what the future may hold for them, while others consult mediums in hopes of communicating with dead loved ones. Terrifying monsters are said to roam the forests outside many cities and towns. Write sociologists Dennis Waskul and Marc Eaton:

> In the 21st century, as in centuries past, stories of ghosts, vampires, and monsters of all kinds both thrill and terrify us, inviting us to imagine that our familiar surroundings may be more enchanted than we thought. Despite—or perhaps because of—advanced scientific understanding

of the natural world, people continue to report beliefs and firsthand experiences with supernatural phenomena. The supernatural remains a part of everyday life, and the time has come to acknowledge that such beliefs and experiences are not doomed to extinction.[2]

Certainly, the evidence supports the contention made by Waskul and Eaton that the supernatural has become an integral part of modern culture. In 2022 the Netflix series *Wednesday*, which tells the story of a teenage girl with supernatural powers, instantly became one of the most popular shows on the streaming service. Anybody who is a fan of the long-running FX network series *American Horror Story* looks forward to each season's tales of ghosts and witches. And viewers' interests in vampires have gone beyond the saga of Dracula and the *Twilight* films. Among the most popular vampire-inspired TV shows currently drawing fans are *The Vampire Diaries* and *Legacies*, both on the CW network.

> "The supernatural remains a part of everyday life, and the time has come to acknowledge that such beliefs and experiences are not doomed to extinction."[2]
>
> —Sociologists Dennis Waskul and Marc Eaton

As the evidence suggests, tales of the supernatural have captivated millions of people since well before the initial publication of *Dracula* more than a century ago. And that is why book publishers as well as film and TV producers continually look for new stories about vampires, ghosts, witches, and many other mythical creatures: to feed the public's enormous appetite for stories about the supernatural world.

CHAPTER ONE

THE GHOST HUNTERS

Every autumn, Jaymes White summons interested fans of the supernatural to places in the Canadian city of Toronto that are believed to be haunted. White describes himself as a mentalist—a person who can make contact with ghosts through a ritual known as a séance.

The site chosen for White's 2022 encounter with the spirit world was the Howland Inn, a hotel erected in Toronto in 1847. Residents of the Lambton Mills neighborhood, where the hotel is located, have long reported encounters with ghosts at the inn. According to White, one of the ghosts who appears from time to time in the hotel is the spirit of an armless soldier who rides through the inn on horseback. Nearby residents say they have heard unexplained clanking sounds, which they believe could be the sounds the soldier made while enjoying a drink at the hotel bar. "When he would drink, he would use his teeth because he had no arms. He would have a clanky sound while drinking,"[3] White says.

People who believe in ghosts accept the notion that following the death of a person, that person's spiritual being continues to exist. All the nonphysical characteristics of the person—demeanor, intelligence, and emotions—remain in spiritual form. Moreover, many people believe that it is possible to make contact with ghosts—to see, hear, and even communicate with these spirits.

White called together devotees of the supernatural so that he could conduct a séance at the Howland Inn, summoning ghosts who are said to inhabit the old hotel's rooms and corridors. Mentalists believe that by drawing on the energy of séance attendees, they can make a connection with the spirit world. "We're hoping we can get (guests) to connect to the house, [and] feel something," White says. "(A séance) is what you bring into it. So, it's not about if you're a skeptic [or] if you're a believer, what it's more about is working as a team to do something you've never done before. If they go into it, full feet, jumping as if it were a pool and give it a chance, they'll get something out of it."[4]

Some people believe that it is possible to make contact with ghosts. For instance, mentalists try to make a connection with the spirit world by conducting a séance.

Lincoln's Ghost

Encounters with ghosts, such as those involving the armless soldier at the Howland Inn, have been reported for thousands of years. In the first century CE, the Roman statesman and author Pliny the Younger wrote a letter in which he described the spirit of a bearded, elderly man haunting his home. Some eight hundred years later, a German family reported being terrorized in their home by a poltergeist—a particularly noisy and fearsome spirit—who threw stones at them and started fires in their home. And more than one guest staying in the White House has reported seeing the ghost of Abraham Lincoln wandering through the executive mansion.

One of the most vivid sightings of Lincoln's ghost was reported by Maureen Reagan, the daughter of then-president Ronald Reagan, and her husband, Dennis Revell. In 1986 the author and journalist Joan Gage was invited to a White House dinner attended by several diplomats and political leaders. She recalls the president telling the guests at the dinner that his dog, Rex, had twice barked frantically in the Lincoln Bedroom and then backed out and refused to set foot over the threshold again. And another evening, the president reported that while the Reagans were watching TV, Rex stood up on his hind legs, pointed his nose at the ceiling, and began barking at something invisible overhead. To the Reagans' amazement, President Reagan told the guests, the dog walked around the room, barking at the ceiling.

According to Gage, the president laughed and told the guests, "I might as well tell you the rest."[5] And then he told the guests that his daughter and her husband always stay in the Lincoln Bedroom when they visit the White House. Some time ago, the president told them, Maureen's husband woke up and saw a transparent figure standing at the bedroom window looking out. Then it turned and disappeared. The president said Maureen teased her husband about it for a month. Then, the president continued, when the cou-

10

This photo shows the Lincoln Bedroom in the White House. Some White House guests have reported seeing the ghost of Abraham Lincoln standing at the window.

ple were there another time, Maureen woke up one morning and saw the same figure standing at the window looking out. As President Reagan described it, his daughter could see the trees right through the figure. And then the figure turned and disappeared.

THE SÉANCE

If Maureen Reagan and Dennis Revell did see the spirit of Abraham Lincoln in the White House, then the couple managed to have their ghostly encounters without the help of a mentalist. But many people believe they do need help in opening channels to the spirit world, and so they rely on mentalists like Jaymes White.

Rita DeMontis, a journalist for the *Toronto Sun* newspaper, attended White's séance at the Howland Inn. DeMontis said the experience started when the sixteen participants toured the building, making themselves familiar with its dark hallways and rooms. After the tour, all sixteen participants gathered in a circle. Recalls DeMontis:

We all linked hands in the dark. And—perhaps it was my imagination—but the room went from dark to pitch dark, with a weird blanket of black descending throughout. I wasn't the only one who noticed this. . . .

Suddenly—a small bell on a table in the middle of the room rang loud and clear.

And then we heard a loud crash. There were surprised shouts and people jumped in their seats. At this point, I was gripping the hand of the stranger next to me—and I realized I could feel his heart beating through my fingers.[6]

DeMontis also reported hearing a mirror fall off a wall. She noticed a strong odor drifting through the room. Lights flickered. "I kept hearing the constant chattering of men somewhere in the back of the building—men who sounded like they were having a good time,"[7] says DeMontis. After the séance, DeMontis looked into the history of the Howland Inn and learned that at one point it had been a popular tavern. She wondered whether the voices she heard were the spirits of some of the former tavern customers.

When the séance concluded, DeMontis found herself thoroughly entertained by the experience. She says, "I do love a good haunting, and a chance to witness things you just can't explain."[8]

Ghosts on Campus

Many devotees of the supernatural do not wait for chance encounters or rely on professional mentalists to help them make contact. Rather, they venture out on their own in search of ghosts.

On the campus of Michigan State University (MSU) in East Lansing, about thirty students are members of the college's Paranormal Society. The society holds weekly meetings in which speakers discuss topics such as the existence of angels, visitors from outer space, and other paranormal activity. Once a year the students participate in an active ghost hunt, often on the campus—but at times the search has taken them off campus into the city of East Lansing. In 2022 the annual ghost hunt was staged on November 2, the traditional Day of the Dead, with Paranormal Society members focusing their attention on the school's so-called North Neighborhood, home to some of the oldest student residence halls on campus.

Ghost Hunting on Campus

Michigan State University is not the only American college to feature a paranormal society for students. Among the schools that provide camaraderie to believers in the supernatural are Pennsylvania State University, the University of Rhode Island, Southern Utah University, Ohio State University, the University of Nebraska–Omaha, Drexel University in Philadelphia, the University of California–San Diego, and dozens more.

Many of the paranormal societies stage annual ghost hunts on campus, searching university buildings and other facilities for evidence of supernatural activity. On a recent ghost hunt in the basement of a dormitory on the campus of the University of Rhode Island, for example, the jovial chatter of participants suddenly stopped when a strange, guttural growl arose from the room. "In a fraction of a second, all of us were screaming and running up the stairs," wrote University of Rhode Island student Caitlyn Picard.

Quoted in University of Rhode Island, "Who You Gonna Call?," 2022. www.uri.edu.

Many students brought along various devices to help them capture evidence of supernatural activity, including cameras and sound-recording equipment. Students carried walkie-talkies as they fanned out through the North Neighborhood, so that in the event that some students caught sight of a ghost, they could summon others to the scene.

The pond at the WJ Beal Botanical Garden at Michigan State University is pictured. In 1890, a fire at a lab in the garden killed some students, and many people believe the area to be haunted by their ghosts.

A Glow in the Spirit Box

One notable piece of equipment brought along for the hunt was a device known as a spirit box. Actually, the spirit box is no more than a magnetic field detector—a common instrument that technicians use to detect magnetism in electronic devices. (The degrees of magnetism generated by electronic devices helps technicians determine whether the devices are operating properly.) The magnetic field detector employed by the MSU students features a range of lights from green to red. Supposedly, when a ghost is nearby, the magnetic energy produced by the spirit sparks a reaction in the box, causing the lights in the red scale to illuminate. Cell phones also produce magnetic fields, so all the students were instructed to turn off their phones prior to the ghost hunt to prevent the devices from sparking false readings.

Alas, after the students had traipsed across the North Neighborhood for several minutes, the spirit box failed to detect supernatural activity. But the students pushed on, moving the search across campus to the school's botanical garden, which has long been believed to be a haven for local ghosts. The garden was established in the nineteenth century by MSU botanist William James Beal, who stored seeds for the garden in a tiny building. When the building caught fire, Beal is said to have ordered students to run into the burning structure to save the seeds. Some of the students did not make it out alive, and it is believed their ghosts haunt the school's botanical gardens.

As the Paranormal Society members approached a large tree in the garden, a bulb illuminated in the spirit box. The students gathered around the spirit box, buzzing with delight as the bulb provided an orange glow. When they moved the box away from the tree, the light faded, but it strengthened again when they returned to the tree.

Many of the students came away from the ghost hunt convinced that the experience provided proof of supernatural activity on campus. Student Grace MacLaren said that before entering college she harbored an ambition to become a professional ghost hunter. She has come to realize, though, that while she is still devoted to the search for supernatural activity, she would do well to find a more mainstream career to pursue. "When I was younger I always wanted to be a ghost hunter . . . and obviously now that I am older I know those aren't legitimate career paths that I can go on," she says. "But with the club it's sort of a glimpse into a world where that could've been a legitimate career path and it's a lot of fun."[9]

Debunking Ghosts

While many of the MSU students came away from the ghost hunt convinced the orange glow in the spirit box was caused by supernatural activity near the tree, there certainly could have been other causes that prompted the device to recognize a magnetic field. Perhaps the spirit box picked up energy from a nearby Wi-Fi transmitter. Or perhaps a TV cable ran underground through the garden and its magnetic energy was detected near the tree.

There are, in fact, many educators, scientists, engineers, and other professionals who are ready to debunk any evidence of supernatural activity, arguing that a logical explanation for what would appear to be a ghostly presence can always be found. Says science writer Benjamin Radford:

The evidence for ghosts is no better today than it was a year ago, a decade ago, or a century ago. Ultimately, ghost hunting is not about the evidence (if it was, the search would have been abandoned long ago). Instead, it's about having fun with friends, telling ghost stories, and the enjoyment of pretending you are searching the edge of the unknown. . . . Ghost hunters may be spinning their wheels, but at least they are enjoying the ride.[10]

STREAMING GHOST HUNTERS

Not everyone gets a chance to attend a séance at a haunted hotel or search for ghosts on a college campus. Not to worry. There are opportunities galore on streaming services and some cable TV networks. Among the most popular shows are *Haunted* on Netflix, *Paranormal Nightmare* on Amazon Prime, *Ghost Hunters* and *Kindred Spirits* on the Travel Channel, and *Ghost Adventures* on Discovery+.

Ghost Hunters, which debuted in 2004, is among the oldest of the series. The show follows the exploits of ghost hunters Jason Hawes and Grant Wilson as they travel the country, searching for paranormal activity. Says TV critic Erin Sharman Cousins, "What makes [Hawes and Wilson] so successful is undoubtedly the men's use of compelling evidence by way of video footage, electromagnetic field (EMF) readers, sound recordings, and eyewitness accounts—many of which terrified audiences get to see themselves (if they haven't covered their eyes in fear, that is.)"

Erin Sharman Cousins, "10 Paranormal TV Shows to Watch That Will Creep You Out," Collider, May 10, 2022. https://collider.com.

And yet, devotees of the supernatural world say there are too many unknowns and too many stories of ghost encounters to simply discount their existence. Says Rita DeMontis, "Debunkers will tell you there's a reason for every creak and sound in alleged haunted abodes, that it's an old house settling with time, that a person's imagination gets fired up under the right circumstances. . . . Let me believe in ghosts and spirits and things that go bump in the night."[11]

CHAPTER TWO

COMMUNICATING WITH THE DEAD

Staging séances in haunted hotels and traipsing through college campuses searching for magnetic energy may help believers in the supernatural in their quests to make contact with ghosts. But many others prefer a much more personal and private experience that enables them to make contact with deceased family members and friends. To communicate with the deceased, they often turn to mediums—people who believe they possess the ability to speak with spirits.

New York City medium Thomas John believes he had his first experience communicating with the dead at age four, when he encountered the ghost of his grandfather—who died before John was born. John recalls waking up one night and seeing the spirit of his grandfather in his bedroom. "I saw an image—an image I will never forget," he says. "The man was dressed just the way I had seen him in many of our old photographs. I immediately recognized him; I didn't even have to think. I just knew, almost as if I had been waiting for him to appear. I felt like I had prepared for this moment every second of my short four years on this Earth. 'Puppa!' I said out loud."[12]

According to John, since that first meeting with the ghost of his grandfather, he has experienced many other encounters with the spirits of the dead. Over the years he has honed his talents as a medium and is today very much in demand by clients who hire him to make contact with their deceased loved ones. He says, "I connect with the Spirits of those that have departed. Taken together, it's a combination of hearing a lot of voices and seeing a lot of things. People are amazed by it, obsessed by it, confused by it, and always intrigued by it."[13]

> "I connect with the Spirits of those that have departed. . . . People are amazed by it, obsessed by it, confused by it, and always intrigued by it."[13]
>
> —Medium Thomas John

Over the centuries, many people have approached mediums like John, imploring them to open channels with deceased relatives and friends. Among the most prominent believers in the power to communicate with the dead was nineteenth-century English poet Elizabeth Barrett Browning. At the time, the practice was known as spiritualism. Her husband, the poet Robert Browning, refused to believe in the power of opening channels with the deceased and often complained to Elizabeth that she was wasting her time, but she continued to confer with mediums

Mediums are people who are believed to possess the power to speak with spirits. A medium, at left, prepares for a session that her client (right) hopes will result in communication with a person who has died.

in efforts to communicate with the dead. She said, "I don't know how people can keep up their prejudices against spiritualism with tears in their eyes, how [it is] not, at least, thrown on the 'wish that might be true,' and the investigation of the phenomena, by that abrupt shutting in their faces of the door of death, which shuts them out from the sight of their beloved."[14]

OPENING CHANNELS WITH THE DEAD

By the time Elizabeth Barrett Browning was consulting with mediums, practitioners of the art of communicating with the dead had developed specific techniques for contacting spirits. Mediums believe that the spirits of the dead and those who were close to them in life both emit energy. It is the role of the medium to open a channel of communication between them by connecting their energies. Says medium Kellee White, "A medium is someone who is able to communicate with souls on the other side [of death] . . . mediums are sensitive and intuitive enough to hear, feel, and see information coming from the other side."[15]

PSYCHOMETRIC SKILLS CAN BE USEFUL

Mediums say they communicate with the dead by connecting with the energy emitted by their clients. Some mediums are able to find that energy in physical objects that were once owned by the deceased. For this reason, people sometimes bring objects like these to their sessions. Making connections with the deceased through physical objects is known as psychometry.

According to the website askAstrology, which is authored by more than twenty mediums and others possessing paranormal abilities, people who intend to buy homes would do well to hire mediums to tour the homes before the purchase is final. In doing so, the prospective owners may learn secrets about the home the current owners may not wish buyers to know. Says the website, "Even more useful could be the hiring of a psychometric practitioner to go through an older home. . . . Even if everyone safely bought and sold the house, and no deaths occurred during ownership, you might want to see if the psychic echo is one of happiness or unhappiness. Walking barefoot over the floors or running hands along the walls and counters can give a talented psychometric reader a tremendous amount of information that they can share with you."

askAstrology, "Psychometry," June 30, 2022. https://askastrology.com.

This picture depicts poet Elizabeth Barrett Browning and her husband, Robert. Elizabeth believed in the power to communicate with the dead, while her husband did not and complained that she was wasting her time.

Tyler Henry is a California-based medium whose clients include the Kardashian-Jenner family, Sofia Vergara, Rebel Wilson, and Lizzo—among others. Henry explains that prior to a session, he prefers to know very little about his client or the spirit the client desires Henry to contact. In fact, when he meets clients at their homes, he prefers to be driven there by an assistant. According to Henry, as the car approaches the client's home he begins to feel the client's energy—absorbing information about the client and the spirit he intends to contact. "Very often . . . it's those impressions that came through in the car that I know I can rely on more than anything,"[16] he says.

After arriving at the home of the client, Henry takes out a notepad and writes down the thoughts and images that enter his head. Specifically, during this phase of the session, he looks for notes that in some fashion repeat themselves—meaning the energy emitted by the spirit producing those impressions in his brain is particularly strong.

Henry says he relies on all five of his senses—sight, sound, smell, touch, and taste—to help him connect with the energy given off by the spirit. In many of these cases, he says, an odor, sound, or vision may have a direct connection with how the client's friend or family member died. Perhaps the deceased person lost his or her life in an automobile accident. That event might present itself to Henry as a loud, crashing noise. "I might get a very strong vision," he says. "I might get what feels like a song stuck in my head."[17]

Once the connection is made, Henry is then able to relay information about the client's deceased loved ones—hoping to find the answers the client is seeking. In 2022 Henry provided a channel to the deceased relatives of journalist Erin Jensen. During the session, Henry told Jensen that he saw a vision of a red rose. In fact, "Rose" is Jensen's middle name, and it is also the first name of Jensen's deceased grandmother. And then he told Jensen, "I feel almost like my circulation doesn't go to my toes . . . it's bad, somebody literally lost blood flow through the extremities."[18] That comment had meaning to Jensen; her aunt died from compli-

Tyler Henry is pictured participating in an E! Network panel in 2016. Henry is a medium who is based in California. His clients include Lizzo and the Kardashian-Jenner family.

cations of diabetes, a disease that often restricts blood flow to the patient's legs. Henry also advised Jensen to tell all her family members to be tested regularly for cancer. (Soon after the session, Jensen learned that her mother had recently undergone a cancer test after learning that one of her relatives had died of cancer.) Finally, Henry told Jensen that a deceased uncle is troubled about the state of his relationship with his son. At the time of his death, he felt they were on bad terms. "I hope part of the healing today is relaying that message that he's all good, even if maybe [they] are still not resolving things," Henry said. "Because it is important that that comes through for this son."[19]

Later, Jensen told her cousin what Henry had said. The cousin responded that his late father may be troubled by the fact that the family had not yet gotten around to placing a headstone on the father's grave. Jensen said her cousin promised to quickly have a headstone placed on the grave.

Jensen says she left the session convinced that Henry possesses the ability to commune with the dead. She says, "If you believe in an afterlife (and I do) why couldn't spirits have figured out a way to communicate?"[20]

A Rainbow on Their Wedding Day

During Jensen's session with Henry, the medium related messages to the client that he heard through the voices of the spirits. But sometimes, the spirit actually speaks using the voice of the medium. In other words, the medium is possessed by the spirit, who speaks directly through the medium to the client. In such cases, the medium falls into a trance—meaning the mind and body of the medium become a vehicle for the spirit. In many cases the communication is not one-sided. The client is able to talk with the spirit while the spirit is channeled through the medium. Says medium Leah Brock-White, "Some [mediums] choose to undergo possession, acting as a vessel for those spirits needing a human form to communicate with this world.

Many mediums . . . thus are presumably able to share the experiences of those on both sides of the veil."[21]

Thomas John relates that during his sessions with clients, he often finds himself possessed by spirits. He recalls one session with a couple, Jennifer and Josef, who wanted to make contact with their deceased fathers. When they arrived for their session with John, Jennifer and Josef advised the medium that they were planning to get married within a few days and wanted to know whether the spirits of their fathers approved of their wedding. As Jennifer and Josef explained to John, their fathers had been business associates, but a dispute between the two men erupted into an angry quarrel that ended when Jennifer's father drew a gun and shot Josef's father, killing him. Jennifer's father then turned the gun on himself, committing suicide.

John says that when the couple told him that story, he could feel an intense energy between them and soon made contact with their deceased fathers—who were also emitting their own intense paranormal energies. After making contact with the two deceased fathers, John says he told the couple:

> They want you to know that even though they can't be at the wedding, they approve of the marriage. They are shaking hands, and though I feel they had difficulties here on Earth, together on the Other Side these men are friends. They don't disapprove of your wedding. They will send you a rainbow on your wedding day. They will be there. [Jennifer's] father's words flowed through me, instead of just to me. He had taken over my mind and body.[22]

A few days later, Jennifer and Josef exchanged vows and were married. And a week after the wedding, John says, he received a letter from Jennifer thanking him for communicating with the

CHANNELING WITH SPIRITS ONLINE

Many mediums offer to channel spirits for clients over the phone or through online portals such as Zoom. Although they are not in the same room with clients, mediums say they can still capture the energy emitted by the client or the spirit the client hopes to reach. Seeing each other's facial reactions and gestures through an online portal enhances the experience, although technical glitches and disruptions in internet connections can be a problem.

Still, grief counselor Jeri K. Augustus says channeling deceased loved ones through the phone or internet helps many people find closure, knowing their deceased relatives are comfortable in the afterlife. She says:

> Phone readings are more advantageous to both the client and the psychic medium. The reason behind this is you will call from the familiarity of your home. You can take the call while lying in bed, in your garden, or anywhere in your comfort zone. This gives you a sense of safety. . . . Aside from the complete anonymity, there is also the privacy that your home offers. You don't need to keep a lookout and explain why you are in a psychic medium's office if a friend sees you.

Jeri K. Augustus, "Psychic Mediums—Get Guidance in These Uncertain Times," March 29, 2021. www.jewelrykeepsakes.com/psychic-mediums.

spirits of their fathers. Jennifer recalled in the letter that while John was possessed by the spirits of the two fathers, they had promised to send a rainbow for the wedding. Jennifer told John that as the couple exited the wedding ceremony they looked overhead and saw no rainbow. In the letter, Jennifer told the medium:

> I was disappointed that I saw no rainbow . . . on the day of our wedding. I just assumed you might have misheard or misinterpreted something. However, the next night as I thumbed through photographs of Dad, I came upon a rainbow patch wedged between the photographs. I have no idea where it came from. It was really bizarre because my mother, who is still mourning, goes through those pictures at least once a week, and says she has never seen it before, and has no idea where it came from, either. Everything you said was great, but honestly, this was the moment I fully believed.[23]

CLIENTS ARE DESPERATE TO BELIEVE

As the letter from Jennifer illustrates, clients are often made believers by the connections mediums make with their dead relatives and friends. But despite experiences like those related by Jennifer and Josef, psychologists and other scientists are highly skeptical that anyone truly possesses the power to communicate with the dead. Richard Wiseman, a professor of psychology at the University of Hertfordshire in Great Britain, says mediums typically have little trouble convincing their clients that they can make contact with deceased loved ones and friends. The clients, he says, are often desperate to make contact and usually enter the sessions fully ready to believe whatever they are told. So when the medium begins a session by telling clients that he or she can detect the presence of their deceased relative in the room, the clients accept this as true.

> "If you take ghosts, for example, or the notion that you wake up and you see an entity at the foot of your bed, and you can't move, and you think the entity is pulling you down, it in fact tells us a great deal about sleep."[24]
>
> —Psychologist Richard Wiseman

Rational explanations can be found for why mediums think they are channeling the dead. For example, Wiseman says, when Thomas John believed he woke up and saw his deceased grandfather, he may simply have been still asleep and dreaming. Wiseman adds, "If you take ghosts, for example, or the notion that you wake up and you see an entity at the foot of your bed, and you can't move, and you think the entity is pulling you down, it in fact tells us a great deal about sleep. When we're asleep and dream, we're paralyzed. . . . Some of the bizarre imagery . . . can lead to thinking that you're having a ghostly experience."[24]

Clearly, though, people who consult with mediums are convinced that the mediums' talents for communicating with the dead are genuine. Typically, mediums charge several hundred dollars for a single session. Even at such a steep cost, many mediums find that their sessions are booked months in advance. Mediums see themselves as providing important services for their clients, many of whom desire to find the answers to the mysteries their loved ones took to their graves.

CHAPTER THREE

LOOKING INTO THE FUTURE

Drive through any small-town or big-city neighborhood in America and it is likely that at some point in your travels you will see a small shop offering opportunities for customers to find out what the future holds for them. Fortune tellers are a mainstay of many American communities. For a fee, anyone can walk in and be told whether they will find happiness with their spouse, obtain fulfillment in their professional life, or be blessed with children.

MaryLee Trettenero, a fortune teller who practices in Boston, Massachusetts, says she knew from an early age that she was gifted with the ability to look into the future. She says, "Being highly intuitive runs in my family. My mother and grandmother always knew things ahead of time. . . . I was the daydreamer amongst my 5 siblings and not at all interested [in] school. Sometimes, when I studied for exams, I only studied what I intuitively thought would be on the test and I usually got A's and B+'s."[25]

After graduating from college, Trettenero found a job with a hotel chain and for the next ten years traveled across the country, helping hotels organize their front desks, guest services, and housekeeping departments. And during that time, Trettenero says, she often found herself falling back on her skills as a fortune teller, looking into her own future to help her make decisions in her job. Finally, she elected to pursue her childhood dream of being a professional fortune teller, helping clients learn about their futures. She left the hotel business and opened her shop, Boston Intuitive, in her home in the Boston neighborhood of Charlestown. "Kids sometimes stop me and want me to read their future," Trettenero says. "One girl in town (about 10 years old) keeps trying to ask me who she's going to marry. But I never read for a kid without the mom having approved for it first."[26]

Tarot Card Readings

Trettenero and other fortune tellers—who are also known as clairvoyants—use a variety of methods to look into the futures of their clients. Trettenero prefers to use tarot cards. These cards are much like typical cards used to play poker, blackjack, or solitaire, but they do not carry the familiar images of the ace, deuce, jack, queen, king and so on. Rather, they are decorated with images of symbolic figures such as the Hermit, the Emperor, Justice, the Lovers, the Star, the Moon, and others.

When the tarot card reader distributes a particular card to the client, the reader interprets the meaning of the card as related to the client's life and future. According to California-based tarot reader Athena Perrakis, a client dealt the Chariot card from the tarot deck may be told, "When the Chariot appears, change and movement are underway. This is a time for victorious progress, moving forward in ways that align with who you are and how you want to be in the world. The Chariot represents the home that moves, which can be physical relocation."[27] Therefore, the client who is dealt the Chariot card from the tarot deck may find his or her life likely to change for the better—perhaps earning a promotion at work or finding a new, and better, home.

When Trettenero schedules a tarot session, she recommends that the client prepare a list of questions in advance, specifically

covering difficult issues the client may be facing. Once the session begins, Trettenero says, she will call upon her powers of clairvoyance to interpret the cards dealt to the client and how the client can expect the future to unfold. She says to her clients:

> The reading will be divided into two parts. For the first half of the reading, I will become a clear channel for intuitive guidance and information passed on to me from my highly developed psychic subconscious. The second half of the reading will address the list of questions or concerns you've brought with you, if they have not already been tackled. . . .

> Expect the unexpected and keep an open mind. I may focus on a subject that surprises you or catches you off guard. Please remember that you scheduled your reading to gain insights and new perspectives which can often come as a shock.[28]

CASTING A HOROSCOPE

Not all clairvoyants read tarot cards. Some prefer to help their clients see into the future using astrology: predicting a client's future according to the positions of the moon, planets, and stars. Astrology should not be confused with astronomy—the science of studying stars and planets by employing telescopes, satellites, and other scientific equipment. Indeed, astrology is not a science.

To look into a client's future, astrologers first need to know the date and time of birth of the client to determine which signs of the zodiac apply to that client. The zodiac is split into twelve segments, each representing a period of the year and named for a mythical symbol from ancient Greece. For example, a client born between January 20 and February 18 is born under the sign of Aquarius, the ancient Greek water carrier; a client born between July 23 and August 22 is born under the sign of Leo, the lion. And so on for all twelve signs.

Tarot cards are one of the ways that fortune tellers look into the futures of their clients. These cards are decorated with images of symbolic figures such as the Hermit, the Emperor, and the Lovers.

By creating a chart showing the positions of the moon, planets, and stars, the astrologer interprets how those heavenly bodies affect the lives of people born under each sign of the zodiac. This forecast of a client's future is known as a horoscope. The astrologer can provide information on a client's future by determining which celestial bodies appear during the days within the client's sign in the zodiac.

For example, if the orbit of the planet Mars is visible during the time of the year that falls under the sign of Scorpio (the scorpion), the astrologer will know that Mars reflects action and masculine energy. Therefore, the astrologer will know a male client is a person of action. But if the orbit of Mars brings it close to the sun during this period, the power given off by the sun will intensify that energy, which may mean the client can expect a major change in his life. By making this prediction, the astrologer has performed what is known as "casting a horoscope." Says California-based astrologer Narayana Montúfar, "Because there are ten planets and twelve zodiac signs in astrology, the combinations of energies are endless."[29] (Astronomers have determined there are actually nine planets in the solar system; however, astrologers count the sun and moon as planets and do not count the earth as a planet; hence, astrologers make their predictions based on a total of ten planets.)

GUIDED BY THE STARS AND PLANETS

Over the years, many people have flocked to astrologers for insights into their future. Florence Harding, the First Lady during the administration of her husband, President Warren Harding, in the early 1920s, was known to summon an astrologer, Marcia Chaumprey, to the White House for regular sessions. During one of the sessions, the fortune teller—she was known as Madame Marcia—told the First Lady that her husband would not live to complete his term. In fact, Warren Harding died on August 2, 1923—just some seventeen months into his four-year term as president.

In contemporary times, many celebrities have acknowledged that they seek guidance from astrologers, among them the singers Beyoncé and Lady Gaga, actress Selena Gomez, and model

TAYLOR SWIFT AND NUMEROLOGY

One technique used to predict the future is known as numerology—essentially, finding a specific number that numerologists call a person's "life path." To find the number, the numerologist needs to know the client's date of birth. The numerologist will then add up the digits in the birth date to determine the life path number. Using that number, the numerologist can then predict on which dates important events in the client's future may occur—such as a wedding date.

The pop singer Taylor Swift is a dedicated believer in numerology. In fact, her life path number is 13. Swift, who was born on December 13, 1989, explains, "I was born on the 13th. I turned 13 on Friday the 13th. My first album went gold in 13 weeks. My first No. 1 song had a 13-second intro. Every time I've won an award I've been seated in either the 13th seat, the 13th row, the 13th section or row M, which is the 13th letter. It's really weird."

Quoted in YahooLife!, "He Hired a Psychic to Contact His Dead Pig? Which Stars Believe in Clairvoyance, Tarot and Crystals?," May 18, 2022. https://uk.style.yahoo.com.

Kendall Jenner. Lady Gaga, for example, consults an astrologer before planning her tours. An Aries, born on March 28, Lady Gaga is known for her energy and pluck, which astrologers believe is typical of people born under the sign of Aries. She has been advised not to perform when the orbit of the planet Mercury enters the sky around her birthday. Lady Gaga has been known to cancel tour dates when Mercury crosses the sky near her birthday because that crossing is thought to bring bad luck. Says British astrologer Patrick Arundell:

> The hitch is that when Mercury [approaches] it does bring with it certain problems which could make touring traumatic for any singer. Since Mercury governs all transportation and communication issues organizing something as complex as a rock tour can be a bit of a headache and this is likely to be the time when passports disappear, weather adversely effects travel and schedules get mislaid. The shrewd Lady Gaga knows this is the moment when the best laid plans of mice and women can get bogged down in a quagmire of delays, misunderstandings and confusion.[30]

THE OUIJA BOARD

Many fortune tellers prefer not to scan the heavens to help their clients look into their future. Rather, they focus on a much smaller surface—one that is typically made of wood or cardboard, usually measuring less than a couple of feet from edge to edge. This tool is known as the Ouija board. The Ouija board—also known as the talking board or witch's board—is similar to an ordinary game board and features the letters of the alphabet arrayed in two semicircles. Below the letters are the numerals 0 through 9. Finally, the words *yes* and *no* are printed atop the board.

Anyone can buy a Ouija board. Typically, when friends try it out, they lay their fingers atop a planchette. This teardrop-shaped device, usually with a small window in the body, can glide across the board. One of the players poses such questions as "Will I pass chemistry?" or "Should I ask my crush out on a date?" After posing the question, the energy connecting the two players takes over and guides the planchette over the letters of the alphabet, the numbers, and the *yes* and *no* words to provide the answer.

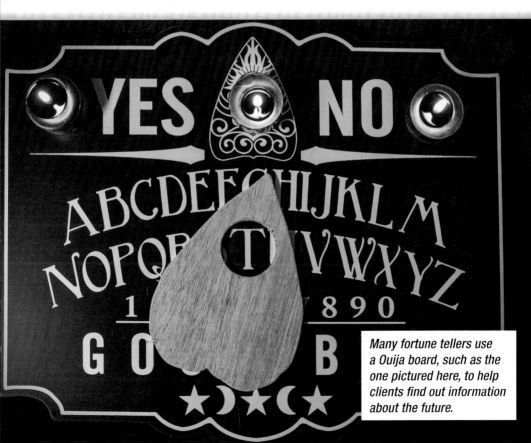

Many fortune tellers use a Ouija board, such as the one pictured here, to help clients find out information about the future.

Clairvoyants caution that Ouija boards work best when someone with the power to tell fortunes is helping the client guide the planchette. Says Joe Loffredo, a fortune teller from Buffalo, New York, "Some [fortune tellers] do work with spirit boards like Ouija. It's good to know that despite what you might hear, it's not a toy, and should not be treated like one. It's best left to those with experience in things spiritual; I definitely do not recommend it for beginners."[31]

Moreover, some fortune tellers insist it is downright dangerous for amateurs to use Ouija boards and that a professional schooled in the techniques of telling fortunes needs to oversee the session. Says Helen Mayor, a fortune teller from Canton, Ohio:

> People need to make the connection that there is nothing mystical about the materials that make up [a] Ouija board that makes it dangerous, it is the intent of what you are trying to achieve through this board game where the danger lays. When you or a group of people focus your energy . . . you may unknowingly be opening up a spirit doorway where you are then unable to control that which comes through. . . .
>
> Many things happen when a person uses the Ouija board. They hear all kinds of noises and or voices. Get a feeling of being watched. Get a sickening feeling in the room where the board was used or a very cold feeling in the room. Worst case is a [dark] spirit comes into the room and terrorizes everyone who comes near the room.[32]

"Many things happen when a person uses the Ouija board. They hear all kinds of noises and or voices. Get a feeling of being watched."[32]

—Fortune teller Helen Mayor

Another method employed to predict the future is palm reading, also known as palmistry. Clients who ask for palm readings simply offer the fortune tellers the palms of their hands. The fortune teller can then draw energy from the palms, deducing from the creases and lines visible

Fortune tellers predict the future for their clients, advising them of coming events in their lives—such as those involving relationships, schoolwork, and jobs. Sarah Wolf, a fortune teller from Austin, Texas, specializes in predicting the future for her clients' dogs.

Wolf uses a deck of tarot cards. (The dog does not sit across the table from Wolf; she deals the cards to the dog's owner.) Wolf says she insists on keeping the tarot readings light; she does not want to unnerve dog owners by advising them that their pets may soon suffer fatal illnesses. She says:

> Some cards have a message for the dog and the dog owner. If someone pulls [the Magician] card, I tell them this card represents a dog with the magical ability to make things happen for themselves and to get what they want. . . . People get nervous. They sit down and they're like, "Oh no, what are the cards gonna say." I tell them we're not gonna say anything bad about your dog. There are a few guidelines: We can ask the cards for some insight or some guidance, but nothing about life or death is allowed. I'll have to remind people the cards don't take the place of your veterinarians.

Quoted in Laura Figi, "7 Questions with Dog Fortune Teller Sarah Wolf," ATX Today, October 12, 2022. https://atxtoday.6amcity.com.

on the surface of the palms information on what the future may hold for a client. Says Aliza Kelly, a New York–based palm reader, "Simply put, palmistry is the art of analyzing the physical features of the hands to interpret personality characteristics and predict future happenings. Within palm reading, hands are considered portals that shed invaluable insight."[33]

> "Simply put, palmistry is the art of analyzing the physical features of the hands to interpret personality characteristics and predict future happenings."[33]
>
> —Astrologer and palm reader Aliza Kelly

A $2 BILLION BUSINESS

Despite the popularity of palmistry, astrology, and other methods of fortune-telling, many scientists believe there is no verifiable way for those techniques to accurately foretell future events. It is true that a fortune teller predicted the death of Warren Harding, but Harding's doctors long suspected that he suffered from a weak heart—the president was known to grow weary very easily. Ultimately, his cause of death was listed as a heart attack. Therefore, while Madame Marcia was able to predict the president's death, it is also likely that his doctors suspected he would soon suffer a fatal heart attack.

Palmistry, astrology, Ouija boards, and tarot cards are all tools employed by fortune tellers to predict what lies ahead for their clients. And there is certainly strong evidence to suggest that clients are very happy with what fortune tellers are relating to them and are eager to come back for more. According to IBISWorld, a Los Angeles, California–based marketing research firm, professional fortune tellers in America collectively earn more than $2 billion a year. Clearly, many people are willing to accept the techniques employed by fortune tellers to help them see what the future may hold for them.

CHAPTER FOUR

THE MAGIC OF WITCHCRAFT

When Cerridwen Greenleaf moved to San Francisco, California, she found herself growing lonely. Knowing very few people in the big city, she longed to make friends and surround herself with people with whom she could share good times.

And so, to cure her loneliness, Greenleaf literally dipped into her bag of tricks. She waited until the new moon—the day of the month when the moon reflects no light from the sun—and then lit a candle, sprinkling some incense over the flame. As the incense burned, Greenleaf chanted an appeal to Freya, a goddess found in Norse mythology. She said:

> I call upon you, friend Freya,
> To fill my life with love and joy. I call upon you, Goddess,
> To bring unto me that which I enjoy
> In the form of people, wise and kind.
> This I ask and give thanks for, blessed be.[34]

According to Greenleaf, soon after casting the spell, her life became full of friends and she no longer had to endure days of loneliness. She says, "I can count on them for boundless love and they bring so much joy to my life."[35]

Greenleaf has practiced witchcraft for many years and since 2013 has written more than twenty books explaining her techniques, the tools she uses, the spells she casts, and the various potions, herbs, oils, and elixirs she employs as a witch. Among the topics covered in her books are spells that can be cast to find love, obtain peace of mind, heal diseases, gain wisdom, help plants grow, and even make food taste better.

Have a crush on a boy at school? According to Greenleaf, the witchy way to attract his attention is to place a pink candle next to a large metal pot. Smear an apple blossom–scented oil onto the candlewick. Place a rose and bell next to the pot. Then, during the night of the full moon, take a thorn from the rose and carve the boy's name into the candle. Light the candle, ring the bell three times, and recite this spell:

I will find true love.
As this candle begins to burn, a lover true I will earn.
As this flame burns even higher, I will feel my lover's fire.[36]

According to Greenleaf, love spells are the most common spells cast by witches—for themselves, certainly, but for others as well. In fact, Greenleaf says, the first spell she cast as a witch—while still a freshman in high school—was intended to help a girlfriend attract the attention of a boy. As things turned out, Greenleaf's friend developed a relationship with the boy, and Greenleaf elected to devote her life to witchcraft.

THE SALEM WITCH TRIALS

The pursuit of witchcraft may have turned out well for Greenleaf, but over the centuries, women as well as men accused of witchcraft have found themselves regarded as truly evil fiends. Such notions led to suspected witches being persecuted, driven from their homes, and often arrested, tried, tortured, and executed.

During the US colonial era, that was the fate that awaited the people accused of witchcraft in Salem, Massachusetts. During the late 1600s a large number of wartime refugees arrived in Salem, having been driven from their homes due to an armed conflict between British and French colonies and their Indian allies. The war was largely fought in portions of the colonies of Massachusetts and New York, as well as in what are today the Canadian provinces of Nova Scotia and Quebec. Many people were displaced by the fighting and fled to regions they hoped would be safe from the warfare. Many of the refugees found their way to Salem.

They were hardly welcomed by the longtime citizens of Salem, who soon blamed the refugees for whatever ills had befallen people in the town. Things came to a boil in 1692 when two young girls started experiencing fits of anger in which they screamed, writhed on the ground, and barked like dogs. Historians suggest the girls may have been afflicted with a mental illness, but in the colonial era modern medical knowledge did not

During the Salem witch trials, many people were accused or convicted of being witches. This picture shows a trial, where a young girl convulses on the floor as the woman she has accused protests to the judge.

exist. But there were plenty of townspeople who liked to gossip, and before long it became evident to the people of Salem what was causing the girls' episodes of hysteria: clearly, these girls were under the spells of witches.

Soon, some twenty-five women and men of Salem were imprisoned on charges of witchcraft. Most denied the charges, but a few confessed—likely under duress during harsh and tortuous hours of questioning. The others went on trial and were found guilty. Twenty of the convicted were executed while five died in prison.

CHANGED ATTITUDES

Centuries ago, witches may have been regarded as truly evil dwellers of the supernatural world, but in modern times witches have found a somewhat more welcoming attitude in American culture. The hit 1939 movie *The Wizard of Oz* featured two witches: a wick-

WITCHES AND THE WORLD CUP

In late 2022 the Argentinian national soccer team shocked the sports world by capturing the World Cup of the International Federation of Association Football, also known as FIFA, during the association's tournament in the nation of Qatar. It is estimated that more than 3.5 billion people worldwide followed the tournament on TV.

Certainly, the Argentinian team was composed of world-class athletes—but the Argentinians may have also had some help from the supernatural world. Hundreds of witches in Argentina conjured up spells to help their country's team. Magalí Martínez, one of the Argentinian witches—known in her country by the Spanish word *brujas*—performed her spells by donning a robe displaying the images of tigers. She then dangled a pendulum over a jersey of the Argentinian team, while nearby she burned cotton that had been doused with the herb mistletoe. As part of the ritual, she chanted a spell. "The pendulum is the most powerful tool I have," she says.

During one of the matches leading up to the championship, Martínez cast a spell she believed would enable Argentinian player Julián Álvarez to score a goal. Four minutes after she cast the spell, Alvarez kicked the ball into the net.

Quoted in Jack Nicas and Ana Lankes, "Behind Argentina's World Cup Magic, an Army of Witches," *New York Times*, December 17, 2022. www.nytimes.com.

This image from the 1939 movie The Wizard of Oz *shows the Wicked Witch of the West (left); Dorothy Gale with her dog, Toto; and Glinda, the Good Witch of the North. In modern times witches have found a more welcoming attitude in American culture.*

ed witch (the Wicked Witch of the West) and a kind-hearted witch (Glinda). The backstories of the two witches were later adapted for a 2003 Broadway musical titled *Wicked*. (A film adaptation is scheduled for release in 2024.) More recently, TV shows such as *Charmed* and *Sabrina the Teenage Witch* depict young girls at-tempting to balance the challenges of their teenage years—dating, homework, relationships with their mortal friends—while honing their supernatural powers as witches. As the adventures of these more modern witches illustrate, in the centuries since the Salem witch trials, witchcraft is no longer regarded by authorities as a crime. Rather, many young people find that performing the rites of witchcraft—such as employing the oils, elixirs, candles, and other tools of the craft—can be uplifting and fun. Many witches practice the rituals of witchcraft alone, but many of them also form covens—small groups of witches who share techniques with one another, learn from each other, and, acting together, cast their spells. And there is also a degree of fun in dressing in the witchy look. Witches often dress all in black, use black eyeliner and lipstick, and have their noses pierced. Says a young witch named Dana, "A witch is, first and foremost, a person in power. . . . To be a witch is to rise against the traditional expectation of gendered conformity and to reclaim the forbidden fruit of individual power and expression. And if that is done via fashion, literature, online covens, or wearing a pointy hat, then that's where it starts."[37]

DIFFERENT TYPES OF WITCHES

Anybody who has seen *The Wizard of Oz* (or *Wicked*) knows that the wicked witch dressed all in black and wore a pointy hat. But the so-called good witch Glinda wore a pink gown and a crown. Not all witches are the same. In fact, witches come in many varieties.

Crystal witches, for example, employ various gems and stones to cast spells, believing they can draw energy out of these hard, rocky substances. Cosmic witches are believers in astrology and time their spells to coincide with what they believe are favorable positions of the sun, moon, planets, and stars. Folk witches are believers in spells and potions that have been used for hundreds of years, believing these original techniques of witchcraft have stood the test of time. Kitchen witches confine their spells to the kitchen, hoping to make food taste a bit better with their magical touches. Green witches employ various plants, flowers, and herbs in their spell casting. Green witches believe they draw their powers from nature.

Canadian witch Paige Vanderbeck says she knew from her earliest experience with witchcraft that she was destined to be a green witch. She says, "One of the first things I've learned about real witchcraft was that it was a path for those who wanted to live in harmony with the earth—those who wanted to grow and harvest plants for magic and medicine, and to honor the spirits of the trees, the animals, and even the rocks around them. I knew right away I'd found the path I was meant to walk."[38]

Ideally, green witches perform their spells outside—surrounded by nature. A green witch known as Kitty offers many spells to help witches achieve their dreams and desires. For example, if a witch needs help in achieving her goals, such as obtaining a new job, she suggests the witch wait until the new moon, then take a few strands of hair (finding them in a brush will work) out to a garden along with a cup of water. The witch finds a plant in bloom. Next, the witch kneels next to the plant, wraps the strands of her hair around the stem, covers the hair with dirt, and finally douses the hair and stem with water. And then the witch chants this spell: "With each inch you grow, with each seed I sow, my dream manifests and comes true." Two weeks later, during the night of the full moon, the witch needs to return to the plant and snip off a leaf or petal. And then, when the witch goes for that job interview or whatever task she needs to accomplish, she takes the leaf or petal with her in a small bag. Says Kitty, "Carry it on you . . . until your dream's manifestation comes to light. Once your dream manifests, bury your spell bag in your garden or yard."[39]

Crystal witches cast spells by using various gems and stones, believing that they can draw energy out of these substances.

WITCHCRAFT ON SOCIAL MEDIA

Statistics would indicate that, as Kitty suggests, many people do believe that magical petals or leaves in their spell bags may very well help them achieve their desires. A 2022 study by the international polling firm Statista found that 21 percent of Americans—about 66 million people—believe in the power of witchcraft. Activity on social media sites would seem to support that statistic. On Facebook, dozens of groups, some with several thousand followers, are devoted to witchcraft. One of the most popular is the Witch Friends group, where members post advice on the types of spells they find most successful, how to organize magic herbs and potions, and how to fashion pendants used in magical rituals.

Meanwhile, among the most popular groups on Instagram are Witches of Insta, with more than five hundred thousand followers; Witch of the Forest, also with more than five hundred thousand followers; and the Hood Witch, with more than three hundred thousand followers. Dozens of self-described witches have created You-

WHO ARE THE WICCANS?

Many people who practice witchcraft regard themselves as members of a religious faith known as Wicca. In addition to casting spells and performing other magical rituals, Wiccans also worship deities—both male and female. (The female deity is known as Mother Goddess; the male is known as the Horned God.) Wiccans do not attend services in houses of worship, and therefore, they largely worship on their own—although the internet has provided Wiccans with portals in which they can connect. Some eight hundred thousand Americans are believed to practice Wicca. Says Helen Alice Berger, a sociologist at Brandeis University in Waltham, Massachusetts, who has studied Wicca:

> Most Wiccans practice magic, which they believe taps into a spirit world often referred to as the "otherworld." Others think of magic as drawing on an energy field they view as surrounding all of us. They do magic to heal themselves and others or to find a new home or job, among other things, and emphasize that magic must not cause harm. Magic is viewed as changing the practitioners as much as their circumstances, encouraging adherents to pursue self-growth and self-empowerment.

Helen Alice Berger, "What Is Wicca? An Expert on Modern Witchcraft Explains," Brandeis University, September 17, 2021. www.brandeis.edu.

Tube channels, where they regularly upload instructional videos on how to cast spells.

One YouTube witchcraft star is Viv Bennett, a college student from Austin, Texas, whose YouTube channel, titled Lunar Faery Witch, has some thirty-eight hundred subscribers. Bennett, who has been practicing witchcraft since age twelve, has produced videos for her followers advising them how to employ "protection magick," which includes spells and charms that would shield them from wrongdoing by people who mean them harm, as well as how to formulate potions, salves, and oils used in spell casting. A few of her videos are devoted to answering questions submitted by her followers on various topics, among them how to balance practicing witchcraft with other aspects of one's life, such as schoolwork (witches need to keep things in perspective and find the time to live in the modern world); how to uncover information on little-known magical spirits (she recommends several books and other sources); and whether she has ever encountered a ghost (yes, in a shopping mall.)

Frustrated by Life's Challenges

And yet Anne-Maria Makhulu, a professor of anthropology at Duke University in Durham, North Carolina, counters that people often turn to a belief in witchcraft when they find themselves frustrated by the challenges of life in the twenty-first century. Perhaps, she says, they are failing in school or unable to achieve satisfaction in their professional lives. As a result, they look for help outside the normal channels of society and arrive at the conclusion that perhaps magic is the answer. "We live in a bewildering world where we don't have a lot of control. And we can imagine doing things through magic that we can't do as ordinary human beings," says Makhulu. "When people say they believe in magical forces, they believe in magic that can make the world equal and just in circumstances where it's not. . . . Witchcraft is about recuperating what is ethical, just and moral."[40]

Bennett concedes that her methods and visions would never stand up to the type of skepticism offered by Makhulu. Nevertheless, she stands by her craft. "Not everything has to be scientific, for now. It's not a prerequisite in order for it to be real or helpful," Bennett says. "There's this idea that we've tested everything through the scientific method. But not everything needs to be viewed through an empirical lens."[41]

Bennett as well as Cerridwen Greenleaf and other witches believe that the spells they cast will lead to happiness for themselves and others. Whether they draw their magic out of nature or feel empowered by the movement of the stars and planets or simply hope to make the meals they cook taste a bit zestier, today's witches believe they have found acceptance and a purpose in the modern world.

CHAPTER FIVE

CRYPTOZOOLOGY AND THE SEARCH FOR MONSTERS

In 1978 residents of the small town of Minerva, Ohio, grew frightened when reports surfaced that several members of the community had been attacked by an unusual predator. Minerva resident Howe Cayton, who was just a teenager at the time, recalls that the attacks started when someone—or something—started hurling rocks at the roof of his family's home. And then several neighbors reported a pounding on their windows. Cayton's neighbor was struck in the face with a rock. Cayton said his family's dog was so frightened that she dug a deep hole in the backyard so she could hide from the commotion. The family later found the dog—dead inside the hole. "She got scared, dug a tunnel in the ground about six feet deep, where something broke her neck,"[42] says Cayton.

The mysterious predator that terrorized the town's residents became known as the Minerva Monster. Decades later, filmmaker Seth Breedlove learned about the case as he was preparing to film a series of movies about supernatural predators. In 2021 Breedlove and members of his crew traveled to Minerva. After they had hiked into the woods to set up their cameras and sound equipment, Breedlove recalls,

> While we were there, we had some really strange things happen. We heard footsteps running through the woods at night and what they call tree knocks, which is basically something hitting a stick on a tree and rocks thrown and all sorts of stuff that didn't make a lot of sense where we were. Because where we were, there weren't really other people.
>
> And then the next day, we were out setting up trail cameras and we were crossing a "pipeline," which is basically a clearcut up the side of a hill. It was a wooded hill where there's like this clearing that ran up the hill. We were in an ATV; we crossed the pipeline up the hill and there was a classic hair-covered "Bigfoot" running across the pipeline! So, I kind of freaked out for a second and jumped out of the ATV as it was moving and attempted to get footage but by then it had already crossed into the trees. . . . It was this real brief moment where I saw something upright, hairy running through the woods. It was broad daylight too, so that probably counts for something.[43]

WHAT IS CRYPTOZOOLOGY?

In the above quote, Breedlove refers to a creature known as Bigfoot. Sightings of this creature first surfaced in the 1950s in Northern California. Witnesses described the creature as a large, hairy beast walking upright much like a human. The creature earned the name Bigfoot due to the very large size of the footprints discovered by investigators. The descriptions of Bigfoot closely matched sightings of a similar

"It was this real brief moment where I saw something upright, hairy running through the woods. It was broad daylight too, so that probably counts for something."[43]

—Filmmaker Seth Breedlove

Bigfoot, as depicted here, earned its name from the large footprints discovered by investigators in California in the 1950s. Bigfoot is believed to be a large, hairy beast that walks upright like a human.

creature first made in the Pacific Northwest in 1811 by British explorer David Thompson, who named the creature Sasquatch. In naming the creature, Thompson used a word from the language of the Indigenous people of the region, meaning "wild men." Moreover, the descriptions of the Sasquatch—and later Bigfoot— closely match descriptions made by explorers in the Himalayan Mountains in Asia. Those explorers named the creature the Yeti, a word drawn from the Tibetan language that basically means "big, hairy creature."

Given the descriptions of these creatures, it can certainly be suggested that there is a connection among all of them—the Minerva Monster, Bigfoot, Sasquatch, Yeti, and others. All of these creatures fall into a class of creatures known as cryptids. They are studied under an area of research known as cryptozoology— essentially, the search for creatures that are otherwise regarded as supernatural.

WELCOMING THE MOTHMAN

Decades after the attacks by the Minerva Monster, citizens of Minerva, Ohio, remain unnerved by the possible presence of the creature in their community. But that is not how citizens of Point Pleasant, West Virginia, regard a creature known as the Mothman. It was first reported in 1966, and during the ensuing decades citizens of Point Pleasant have told of seeing a 10-foot-tall (3.3 m) creature with huge wings and the head of an insect. Says Point Pleasant resident Carolin Harris, "I definitely know the Mothman is real."

Rather than live in fear of the Mothman, though, residents of Point Pleasant have embraced the creature. A statue created in the image of the Mothman has been erected in the center of town. Moreover, each September the town stages the Mothman Festival, featuring parades—participants dress up in Mothman costumes—as well as concerts, lectures, and tours of locations in Point Pleasant where witnesses have reported sightings of the cryptid.

Quoted in Fallon Pierson, "Man Photographs Creature That Resembles Legendary 'Mothman' of Point Pleasant," WCHS TV 8, November 21, 2016. https://wchstv.com.

Cryptozoologist Loren Coleman has been gathering evidence of cryptids for more than sixty years. He started his quest at age fourteen, when he found himself enthralled with the story of the Yeti. During his career he has searched for evidence of cryptids in all fifty states as well as several foreign countries and established the International Cryptozoology Museum in Portland, Maine, to display the evidence he has uncovered. Says Coleman:

> I have chased monsters . . . tracked down teleported animals, interviewed scores of people who have seen creatures from mysterious kangaroos to black panthers, or viewed entities from phantom clowns to lake monsters, and more. . . . My car has crisscrossed the Midwest so many times that sometimes I think I could turn it loose and it would steer itself to the latest Bigfoot or panther sighting. I find myself going to places like Fort Mountain, Georgia, and Mystery Hill, New Hampshire, to examine strange structures built by ancient unknown peoples, or to various wooded areas in the Northeast to run down the latest phantom feline account.[44]

FROM CYCLOPS TO GODZILLA

Monsters like Bigfoot and the Yeti were a part of popular culture long before cryptozoologists started hunting for evidence of their existence. During the era of ancient Greece, cryptids were common characters in fiction and folklore—among them Cyclops, a giant with a single eye situated in its forehead; the Minotaur, a beast that was half human and half bull; and the Centaur, a creature that was half human and half horse. Also, Medusa was imagined as a winged woman with snakes growing out of her head in the place of hair. It was said that anyone who gazed at Medusa would turn to stone. Among the other mythical creatures that surfaced in folklore over the ensuing centuries were ogres, giants, mermaids, dragons, and unicorns.

These creatures—and many others—have remained a part of twenty-first century culture. For example, in 2014 a Hollywood studio produced a new version of the film *Godzilla* that earned more than $200 million at the box office. Godzilla is a mythical giant reptile that tramples cities while shooting fire out of its mouth. The 2014 production was a remake of a movie originally released in 1954 by Japanese filmmakers. The fact that the new version drew millions of fans into theaters sixty years after its original debut illustrates people's enduring fascination with cryptids.

Creatures like Godzilla have remained part of the culture of the twenty-first century. This movie poster, from the 2014 remake of Godzilla, *earned more than $200 million at the box office.*

THE LOCH NESS MONSTER

Among the most familiar cryptids that literally surfaces from time to time is known as the Loch Ness Monster—a giant serpent that has been sighted swimming in Loch Ness, a freshwater lake in Scotland. Reported sightings of the monster—known familiarly as Nessie to residents of the Loch Ness region—date back as far as 565 CE. In the centuries that followed, many cryptozoologists have crept into the marshes surrounding the loch in search of evidence of Nessie.

A breakthrough of sorts occurred in 2022 when a team of scientists found evidence suggesting that an amphibian dinosaur known as a plesiosaur was able to survive in freshwater lakes. Prior to that discovery, it was believed that plesiosaurs lived in saltwater oceans only.

The significance of that finding sparked hope among crypto-zoologists that Nessie could be a plesiosaur and that the offspring of the dinosaur have survived for millions of years and are still living in Loch Ness. (A famous photograph snapped in 1934 shows a dark and fuzzy image of Nessie, whose long neck and tiny head closely resemble those of a plesiosaur.) Reported the University of Bath, a British college that helped sponsor the research into the plesiosaur, "What does this mean for the Loch Ness Monster? On one level, it's plausible. Plesiosaurs weren't confined to the seas, they did inhabit freshwater."[45]

Still, the university also pointed out that plesiosaurs are believed to have died out some 66 million years ago, and geological studies of the region have found that Loch Ness was formed just some 10,000 years ago. Therefore, had a few plesiosaurs somehow survived the extinction of the species, they would have had to find someplace else to live for millions of years until, finally, water surged into the region of Scotland where the loch is located.

And yet each year several people report sightings of the monster. An organization known as the Official Loch Ness Monster Fan Club keeps track of the sightings and reports that more than

THE WEREWOLF OF AMARILLO

Werewolves are said to be humans who turn into wolves while still retaining some human qualities, such as the ability to walk upright. Stories of bloodthirsty werewolves date back to ancient Greece. Perhaps the most famous werewolf in popular fiction is Lawrence Talbot, the central character in the 1941 horror movie *The Wolfman*. (A new version of the film was released in 2010.) According to the story, Talbot turns into a werewolf after he is attacked by another werewolf.

Many people in Amarillo, Texas, have come to believe that werewolves are not just characters in Greek mythology or contemporary horror films. In 2022 a security camera at the Amarillo Zoo recorded footage of a strange creature. (The camera was aimed outside the zoo's security fence.) The camera recorded an image of a canine-like creature, about the size of a human, walking on two feet. Said Michael Kashuba, director of the Amarillo Parks and Recreation Department, "I think it's exciting to see the interest in something like this. It's obviously out of the norm for us."

Quoted in Nick Mordowane, "Werewolf or a Costume: Creepy Figure Filmed Outside Zoo Puzzles Internet," *Newsweek*, June 8, 2022. www.newsweek.com.

eleven hundred people have told of seeing Nessie since that first sighting in 565 CE. A bird-watcher who visited Loch Ness in 2022 provided this account of his sighting:

> I saw a large animate object in the water between both banks of the loch at approximately 9.30 a.m. It was dark in color and stayed there for around 20 seconds before sinking into the water. I watched it with binoculars that I'd taken with me in the hope of seeing ospreys that had recently returned to the area. It was difficult to estimate the size but it was definitely larger than a seal and given the angle, there may have been two, one behind the other.[46]

THE JERSEY DEVIL

If undeniable evidence surfaces identifying the Loch Ness Monster as a modern-day plesiosaur, chances are Nessie could be very frightening. Plesiosaurs are believed to have been carnivores—meat eaters—meaning that cryptozoologists would do well to exercise caution as they approach the creature.

Certainly, the same level of caution should be exercised if cryptozoologists find themselves facing other supernatural creatures, such as Bigfoot or the Yeti. And without question, abundant caution should be exercised should anyone find themselves face-to-face with a creature known as the Jersey Devil.

The Jersey Devil is reported to be an inhabitant of a rural portion of eastern New Jersey known as the Pine Barrens. According to Tea Krulos, an author who has written extensively on cryptozoology, "First reported in the Pine Barrens forests of New Jersey in the 1700s, witnesses described the creature as a horse-faced, bat-winged, devil-tailed creature."[47] According to legend, the Jersey Devil is the cursed child of a colonial woman named Deborah Leeds who, while giving birth to her thirteenth child, called on the devil to ease the pain of childbirth. The devil responded to the mother's pleas by turning the child into a hideous monster.

From time to time, sightings of the Jersey Devil are reported. In October 2022 a witness posted a video of an unusual creature on an Instagram page known as Mysteries Unexplained. The witness recorded a brief cell phone video while traveling through the Pine Barrens. The video shows a silhouette of a four-legged creature with a round head and bat-like wings perched on the branch of a tree. After a few seconds the creature spreads its wings and flies away.

SKEPTICISM FROM SCIENTISTS

As cryptozoologists continue to search for evidence of the Jersey Devil as well as Bigfoot, the Loch Ness Monster, and other cryptids, they invariably face skepticism from the scientific community. Biologists, zoologists, anthropologists, and others who study life on earth do not regard cryptozoology as a true science but rather as a phony area of research known as pseudoscience. Says Krulos:

Cryptozoology stands at the intersection of folklore and fact. Thus, it serves multiple functions for various audiences. For those who simply "want to believe," the allure is in the mystery surrounding eyewitness reports and conflicting claims. For more serious cryptozoologists, the thrill is quite the opposite: they hope to make a breakthrough discovery by use of scientific methods of data collection. Cryptozoologists dream that, after enduring years of ridicule from mainstream science, they will have the last laugh when their dogged research uncovers definitive proof of the existence of cryptids.[48]

And yet, even in the face of such skepticism, cryptozoologists continue to press on. Loren Coleman says the work of cryptozoologists has established that many animals that were once believed to be cryptids have been verified as real. Among those animals, he says, are the panda, Komodo dragon (a large lizard), and megamouth shark. Says Coleman:

> "Cryptozoologists dream that, after enduring years of ridicule from mainstream science, they will have the last laugh when their dogged research uncovers definitive proof of the existence of cryptids."[48]
>
> —Author Tea Krulos

Cryptozoology is the study of animals of which there are documented sightings, but which are as yet unknown to science. Some people call it a pseudoscience, but I object to that terminology. I'm not interested in ghost stories or UFOs. They're like a wisp of smoke. I like biological cases where I can find real evidence beyond testimony, such as hair, footprints or photographs. . . . The goal of cryptozoology is to discover new species.[49]

After decades of investigation by cryptozoologists, there is still virtually no significant proof that supports the notion that Bigfoot, the Minerva Monster, the Loch Ness Monster, or the Jersey Devil do exist. Other than vague reports by witnesses, the discovery of some very large footprints, and perhaps a few fuzzy and unfocused seconds of the creatures caught on grainy film

> "The goal of cryptozoology is to discover new species."[49]
>
> —Cryptozoologist Loren Coleman

footage, little real evidence has surfaced that can positively prove the existence of these monsters. And yet reports of cryptids continue to surface in modern society—more than eleven hundred have been reported for the Loch Ness Monster alone. And so cryptozoologists will keep looking for evidence, believing that one day they will provide legitimate proof that these monsters are real.

SOURCE NOTES

Introduction: The Vampire Tourists

1. Rita Cook, "Transylvania: A Walk in Dracula's Shadow," Travelers Way, August 11, 2011. https://thetravelersway.com.
2. Dennis Waskul and Marc Eaton, eds., *The Supernatural in Society, Culture, and History*. Philadelphia: Temple University Press, 2018, p. 1.

Chapter One: The Ghost Hunters

3. Quoted in Brian Baker, "Toronto's Historic Lambton House Chosen for Jaymes White's Sixth Annual Séance," Superstitious Times, September 18, 2022. www.superstitioustimes .com.
4. Quoted in Baker, "Toronto's Historic Lambton House Chosen for Jaymes White's Sixth Annual Séance."
5. Quoted in Joan Gage, "Ronald Reagan's White House Ghost Story," HuffPost, December 13, 2013. www.huffpost.com.
6. Rita DeMontis, "My Scary Seance Experience Turned into a Howling Success," *Toronto Sun*, October 31, 2022. https:// torontosun.com.
7. DeMontis, "My Scary Seance Experience Turned into a Howling Success."
8. DeMontis, "My Scary Seance Experience Turned into a Howling Success."
9. Quoted in Jaden Beard, "Inside a Ghost Hunt with MSU Paranormal Society," *State News* (Michigan State University), November 2, 2022. https://statenews.com.
10. Benjamin Radford, "The Shady Science of Ghost Hunting," Live Science, October 21, 2022. www.livescience.com.
11. DeMontis, "My Scary Seance Experience Turned into a Howling Success."

Chapter Two: Communicating with the Dead

12. Thomas John, *Never Argue with a Dead Person: True and Unbelievable Stories from the Other Side*. Charlottesville, VA: Hampton Roads, 2015. Kindle edition.

13. John, *Never Argue with a Dead Person*.
14. Quoted in Karen, "Elizabeth Barrett Browning: Poet and Spiritualist," Spiritual Path Spiritualist Church, January 18, 2022. https://spiritualpathspiritualistchurch.org.
15. Quoted in Kimberly Zapata, "Mediums Don't Actually 'Talk' to the Dead," Oprah.com, 2022. www.oprah.com.
16. Quoted in Charlotte Walsh, "So, How Does Tyler Henry Talk to the Dead?," Netflix, March 11, 2022. www.netflix.com.
17. Quoted in Erin Jensen, "Is Tyler Henry for Real? An Honest Account of a Reading by the 'Life After Death' Medium," *USA Today*, March 11, 2022. www.usatoday.com.
18. Quoted in Jensen, "Is Tyler Henry for Real?"
19. Quoted in Jensen, "Is Tyler Henry for Real?"
20. Jensen, "Is Tyler Henry for Real?"
21. Quoted in Zapata, "Mediums Don't Actually 'Talk' to the Dead."
22. John, *Never Argue with a Dead Person*.
23. John, *Never Argue with a Dead Person*.
24. Quoted in Kylie Sturgess, "Interview with Professor Richard Wiseman," *Skeptical Inquirer*, August 10, 2011. https://skepticalinquirer.org.

CHAPTER THREE: LOOKING INTO THE FUTURE

25. Quoted in BostonVoyager, "Meet MaryLee Trettenero of Boston Intuitive in Charlestown," June 12, 2017. http://bostonvoyager.com.
26. Quoted in *Charlestown Patriot-Bridge* (Revere, MA), "When You Know, You Know," April 12, 2012. http://charlestownbridge.com.
27. Athena Perrakis, "What Is Tarot?," Sage Goddess, 2021. www.sagegoddess.com.
28. MaryLee Trettenero, "Tips for a Successful Psychic Tarot Reading," Boston Intuitive, 2023. www.bostonintuitive.com.
29. Narayana Montúfar, "How to Read Your Birth Chart, According to a Professional Astrologer," *Women's Health*, June 28, 2022. www.womenshealthmag.com.
30. Patrick Arundell, "Lady Gaga and Mercury Retrograde," Patrick Arundell personal website, 2023. www.patrickarundell.com.
31. Quoted in Quora, "Do Psychic Mediums Use Ouija Boards?," 2018. www.quora.com.
32. Quoted in *Canton (OH) Repository*, "Ghosts, Ouija Board and Séance: Things You Need to Know," October 18, 2012. www.cantonrep.com.
33. Aliza Kelly, "A Beginner's Guide to Reading Palms," *Allure*, December 2, 2021. www.allure.com.

Chapter Four: The Magic of Witchcraft

34. Cerridwen Greenleaf, *5-Minute Magic for Modern Wiccans*. New York: Ryland Peters & Small, 2022. Kindle edition.
35. Greenleaf, *5-Minute Magic for Modern Wiccans*.
36. Cerridwen Greenleaf, *The Practical Witch's Love Spell Book: For Passion, Romance, and Desire*. New York: Running, 2021, p. 8.
37. Quoted in Ellen Ricks, "How to Dress like a (Real) Witch," Byrdie, June 23, 2022. www.byrdie.com.
38. Paige Vanderbeck, *Green Witchcraft: A Practical Guide to Discovering the Magic of Plants, Herbs, Crystals, and Beyond*. Emeryville, CA: Rockridge, p. ix.
39. Quoted in Other Worldly Oracle. "How to Become a Green Witch," November 3, 2018. https://otherworldlyoracle.com.
40. Quoted in Duke University, "Belief in Witchcraft, Magic Serves 'Basic Human Need,' Professor Says," ScienceDaily, October 27, 2007. www.sciencedaily.com.
41. Quoted in Michelle Boorstein, "From Spellcasting to Podcasting: Inside the Life of a Teenage Witch," *Washington Post*, October 28, 2021. www.washingtonpost.com.

Chapter Five: Cryptozoology and the Search for Monsters

42. Quoted in Suzanne Stratford, "What Was It? Man Talks About 'Minerva Monster' Mystery 40 Years Later," Fox 8, October 31, 2017. https://fox8.com.
43. Quoted in Michelle Swope, "On the Hunt for the Unexplained with 'Small Town Monsters' Creator Seth Breedlove," Bloody Disgusting, July 12, 2022. https://bloody-disgusting.com.
44. Loren Coleman, *Mysterious America: The Ultimate Guide to the Nation's Weirdest Wonders, Strangest Spots, and Creepiest Creatures*. New York: Paraview, 2007, p. 13.
45. Quoted in Cassidy Ward, "Discovery of Freshwater Plesiosaurs Makes Loch Ness Monster 'Plausible,'" SYFY, July 28, 2022. www.syfy.com.
46. Quoted in Official Loch Ness Monster Sightings Register, "Sightings at Loch Ness from 2021 On," 2022. www.lochnesssightings.com.
47. Quoted in Waskul and Eaton, eds., *The Supernatural in Society, Culture, and History*, p. 201.
48. Quoted in Waskul and Eaton, eds., *The Supernatural in Society, Culture, and History*, p. 207.
49. Loren Coleman, "'I'm the World's Foremost Cryptozoologist,'" *Financial Times*, March 10, 2017. www.ft.com.

FOR FURTHER RESEARCH

Books

Alysa Bartha, *Essential Tarot Mastery: A Comprehensive Tarot Reader's Guide*. Hillsburgh, ON, Canada: Acillea Fortuna, 2022.

Louise Edington, *The Complete Guide to Astrology: Understanding Yourself, Your Signs, and Your Birth Chart*. New York: Rockridge, 2020.

Cerridwen Greenleaf, *Wiccan Moon Magic: Spells and Rituals to Harness Lunar Energy for Wellbeing and Joy*. New York: CICO, 2022.

Mary-Anne Kennedy, *How to Become a Medium: A Step-by-Step Guide to Connecting with the Other Side*. New York: Library Tales, 2022.

J.W. Ocker, *The United States of Cryptids: A Tour of American Myths and Monsters*. Philadelphia: Quirk, 2022.

Internet Sources

Michelle Boorstein, "From Spellcasting to Podcasting: Inside the Life of a Teenage Witch," *Washington Post*, October 28, 2021. www.washingtonpost.com.

Rita DeMontis, "My Scary Seance Experience Turned into a Howling Success," *Toronto Sun*, October 31, 2022. https://torontosun.com.

Aliza Kelly, "A Beginner's Guide to Reading Palms," *Allure*, December 2, 2021. www.allure.com.

Narayana Montúfar, "How to Read Your Birth Chart, According to a Professional Astrologer," *Women's Health*, June 28, 2022. www.womenshealthmag.com.

Michelle Swope, "On the Hunt for the Unexplained with 'Small Town Monsters' Creator Seth Breedlove," Bloody Disgusting, July 12, 2022. https://bloody-disgusting.com.

WEBSITES

askAstrology
https://askastrology.com

Visitors to the website can receive daily predictions for the future by clicking on one of the signs of the zodiac, which appear on the site's home page. Other features of the website include explanations of tarot readings, numerology, how to create channels with the spirits of the dead, psychometry, palmistry, and Ouija boards.

Bran Castle
www.bran-castle.com

The website features a virtual tour of the medieval-era castle in Romania that author Bram Stoker imagined as the home for the vampire Dracula. Visitors can find tabs for "The Myth of Count Dracula" as well as other creepy occupants of the castle, among them ghosts, werewolves, and a Romanian cryptid known as the Strigoi—an evil spirit said to rise from the grave.

International Cryptozoology Museum
https://cryptozoologymuseum.com

The Portland, Maine, museum is maintained by American cryptozoologist Loren Coleman to display the evidence he has found in his search for cryptids. The collection includes supposed hair samples from Bigfoot and the Yeti. Also featured are sculptures of cryptids based on eyewitness accounts—among them a mermaid and a sea serpent spotted off the coast of British Columbia, Canada.

Small Town Monsters
www.smalltownmonsters.com

Filmmaker Seth Breedlove created this website to chronicle his work in producing films about cryptids in America. Visitors to Breedlove's website can find a trailer for his film, *The Jersey Devil Curse*, as well as numerous podcasts he has produced covering topics such as Bigfoot, Mothman, and werewolves.

Thomas John Celebrity Medium
www.mediumthomas.com

Maintained by New York City–based medium Thomas John, this website includes a Blog tab, where students can read John's commentaries on supernatural topics such as interpreting dreams, speaking with the dead, the roles of clients during their sessions with mediums, and how people can develop their own powers to communicate with the dead.

INDEX